CUENTO
DE LUZ

To my mother, for allowing me to never stop being a child. To Eneko, for being so big, but at the same time never ceasing to be small. To Nívola, for sharing the moon with me. To Mariama, for showing me that dreams can come true.

— Jerónimo Cornelles —

To Pa, Hamadi, and all the women and children I met in Gambia, with their eyes full of purity and hope. And to Africa, which changed my life forever.

— Nívola Uyá —

Mariama: Different But Just the Same

Text © Jerónimo Cornelles
Illustrations © Nívola Uyá
This edition © 2014 Cuento de Luz SL
Calle Claveles 10 | Urb Monteclaro | Pozuelo de Alarcón | 28223 | Madrid | Spain
www.cuentodeluz.com
Title in Spanish: Mariama: Diferente pero igual
English translation by Jon Brokenbrow

ISBN: 978-84-16147-60-1

Printed by Shanghai Chenxi Printing Co., Ltd. May 2014, print number 1434-2

FSC
www.fsc.org
MIX
Paper from
responsible sources
FSC® C007923

MARIAMA
DIFFERENT BUT JUST THE SAME

Jerónimo Cornelles & Nívola Uyá

my grandma

my village: Fulakunda

me

my mom

my dad

This is the story of a little girl named Mariama. One day, her parents told her that she was going to move to a country far, far away.

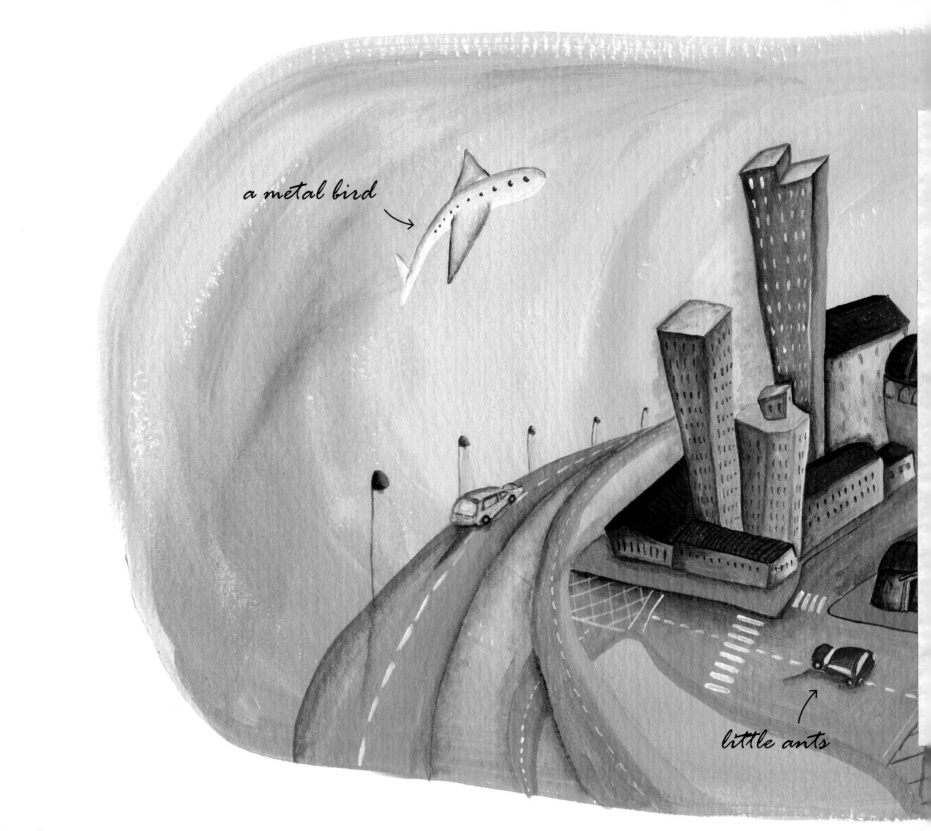

a metal bird

little ants

After a long journey by car, train, boat, and plane
to her new home, everything was different.

There were no animals in the streets; and instead
of earth, there were long, grey tongues.

like a caterpillar

The first days of school weren't easy.

Mariama couldn't understand what the other kids were saying, as they were speaking a very strange language. But what Mariama found especially strange was that the kids were nearly as white as the African moon that shone over the village where she used to live.

The new food was different too,
but it was still nice.

domoda:
my favorite food

Even the things her new classmates used to eat were different: the knives and forks, plates, salt shakers, and toothpicks. Everything was new for Mariama!

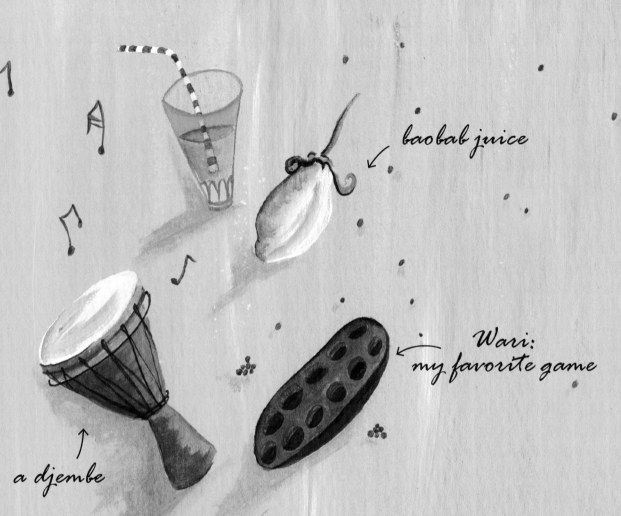

baobab juice

Wari:
my favorite game

a djembe

"You have to try even harder than the rest of your friends, so that you can talk to them," said her mom.

"And what am I supposed to talk to them about?" said Mariama. "Everything's different here, but they think I'm the one that's different."

"Well, you have to tell your new friends that in this great big world, there are lots of other places that we sometimes don't pay any attention to and forget. If you talk about your land, nobody will forget your people."

So Mariama learned the new language.

blah?

It wasn't easy,
but with the help of her new friends Hugo and Paula, she did it.

The most amazing thing for Mariama was discovering that the only difference between her and Hugo and Paula was the color of their skin; and that although they had different customs, they were just the same in every other way.

Black or white, Mariama, Hugo, and Paula were all children.
They were children who wanted to play and laugh…

strawberry
bubble gum

Children who could teach her lots of things
about the new land she lived in…

Children whom she could teach about life in Africa, and the customs of the people who lived there...

farmyard eggs

doves

Children who didn't have to worry about anything else apart from being children.

my friends

Eventually, by working hard and with her friends' help, Mariama learned to love and appreciate her new life.

But even so, when night came, she felt very sad when she remembered the stars in the African sky and the stories her grandma, Isatu, used to tell her.

That was when Mariama remembered what her grandma had told her before she left:

"Every night, wherever you are, when the moon rises, look up at it. I will be looking at it too. Then we will be together, and no land or sea will be able to keep us apart."

DO YOU WANT TO PLAY WITH MARIAMA?

This is what Mariama taught her new friends about Africa:

HOW TO PLAY THE DJEMBE

Africa has a long, rich musical tradition.

For centuries, singers and musicians have preserved the history and identity of their people through songs that are sung to families and tribes.

The djembe is one of Africa's most important instruments.

If you tap the skin close to the center, it makes a deep sound; if you tap it close to the edge, it makes a more high-pitched sound.

HOW TO ENJOY BAOBAB JUICE

The baobab is a beautiful tree from the semi-arid region of central Africa, which can grow to nearly 100 feet high, with a diameter up to 60 feet. Some baobabs are known to be 4,000 years old.

A bittersweet pulp is extracted from the fruit of the baobab, which is used to prepare a delicious, refreshing juice.

AND HOW TO PLAY CREATIVELY

Africa has a long tradition of playing games that offer a great opportunity to learn and have fun.

Creativity and imagination are the key to making toys by recycling materials such as wood, containers, stones, branches and seeds.

Come on, get inspired and make a toy of your own!